This Jacana book belongs to:

....

....

For my daughters Michaelah, Keziah, Aviyah and Raniah – KT

To all the children who were perhaps confused about their heritage,

but have now found a tool that will not only bring understanding,

but will water the seeds of acceptance we all yearn for as people – CG

First published by
Jacana Media (Pty) Ltd in 2020

10 Orange Street
Sunnyside
Auckland Park 2092
South Africa
+2711 628 3200
www.jacana.co.za

ISBN 978-1-4314-2846-5

Set in Liebe Ruth 15pt / 26pt
Job no. 003535

See a complete list of Jacana titles at www.jacana.co.za

I Have Brown Skin and Curly Hair

Written by Karen Theunissen
Illustrated by Charles Gibbons

JACANA CHILDREN'S BOOKS

I have brown skin
and curly hair.

My sister's hair is straight
and her skin is kinda fair.

My brother's curls are tight and his skin is really dark.
My daddy says we're coloured and from Eldorado Park.

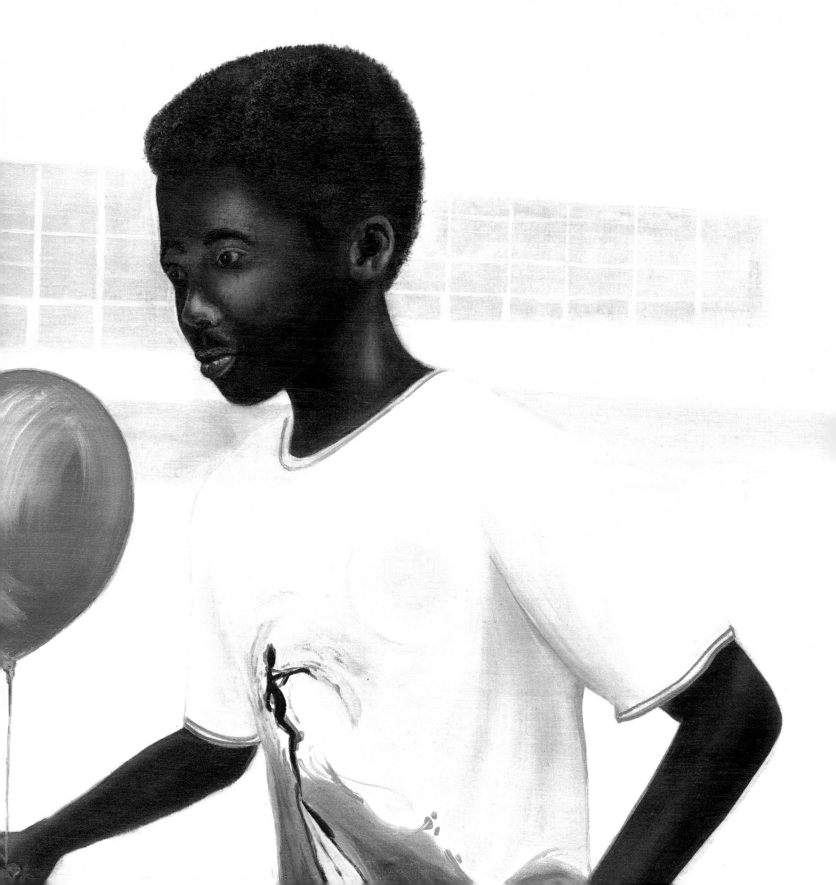

My daddy has a booming voice.
He is strong and tall.
He throws me up in a tumble
and doesn't let me fall.

My mummy is beautiful, with light
brown hair and eyes so green.
She loves to tickle my tummy
and make me laugh and scream.

I see how people look at us when we go out.
They wonder and ask what we're all about.

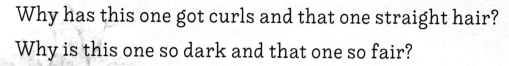

Why has this one got curls and that one straight hair?
Why is this one so dark and that one so fair?

"No one else seems to
struggle like me," she thinks.
"My hair is a crown,
but one made of thorns."

I hear Daddy say,
"It's my great-grandmother
from St Helena's bay.
She crossed the
Atlantic Ocean
on a cold July day."

"She landed at the Cape and from there she made her way.
I am told she was Creole, with long hair, jet black.
Now my daughter's hair looks just like that."

"My great-great-grandfather – from Croatia he came, looking for gold, fortune and fame. I'm told he wore a large hat atop a mass of curls."

"This daughter's hair's the same, with the same kind of twirls."

"But anyhow, it matters not what curly,
twirly or straight hair you've got!
Don't you see? You don't need to look the
same to be family!"

Then they say to Daddy, "I don't mean to pry.
You look very different. May I ask why?"
"My ancestors, they say, were Cape Malay.
Brought from Indonesia, over the waves,
to the Cape to work as slaves.
That part of my history is awfully sad.
Those people who brought them were very bad."

"But anyhow, it matters not what kind of ancestors you've got!
Slave or free, don't you see? You don't need to look the same to be family!"

With curiosity, they look at my mother and frown, and then they ask,
"Is your hair really light brown?"

Mummy says, "Let me tell you what I have been told.
My hair is from my Griqua ancestors of old."

"Griquas?" they ask. "Who were they?"
Then Mummy would say, "They hailed from
the Khoi Khoi a long time ago, who some say
were the first South Africans,
you know? Now the Griquas,
they moved all over the land,
to work it, to build it and earn the rand."

"But anyhow, it matters not
what colour hair you've got!
Don't you see?
You don't need to look the
same to be family!"

"And your eyes, why that green colour?"
Mummy says, "It's from my grandmother.
She lived in Potchefstroom and was an Afrikaner.
My mum was a seamstress, my dad was a farmer.
They all had green eyes, that's the answer."

"But anyhow, it matters not what colour
eyes you've got! Don't you see?
You don't need to look the same to be family!"

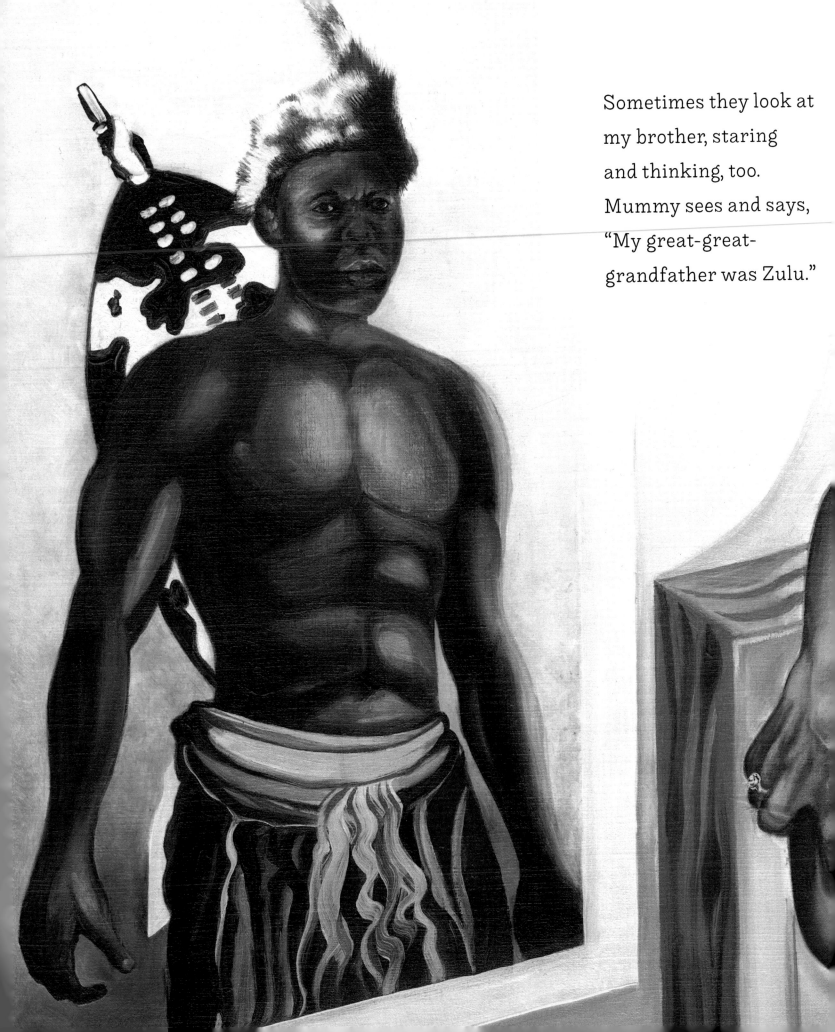

Sometimes they look at my brother, staring and thinking, too. Mummy sees and says, "My great-great-grandfather was Zulu."

"He was a warrior, strong with might. He put fear in all men at first sight. He had ebony skin and was the tallest in a crowd. My son takes after him and he makes me so proud."

"But anyhow, it matters not what
colour skin you've got! Don't you see?
You don't need to look the same to be family!"

They look at my curly hair and smile,
and then they go quiet for a while.
I look up bravely and say,
"This is why we all look this way!"

"But anyhow, it matters not what kind of look I've got!
Don't you see? I'm unique, free to be me!
We all look different but we're one family!"